This story belongs to:

Property of Panola
Campus

TRINITY BASIN
P R E P A R A T O R Y

Little Moon

Story & Pictures by Megan Padalecki

For the moon that shines for someone every night
and for Ryan, who shines just for me.
– M.P.

Publisher's Cataloging-In-Publication Data
(Prepared by The Donohue Group, Inc.)

Names: Padalecki, Megan, author, illustrator.
Title: Little Moon / story & pictures by Megan Padalecki.
Description: First edition. | [San Francisco, CA] : PadaleckiStudio.com, 2016. | Interest age
    level: 004-008. | Summary: "A young squid discovers her unique talents as she
    journeys through dangerous ocean environments to find her way home."--Provided
    by publisher.
Identifiers: LCCN 2016910189 | ISBN 978-0-9977352-0-8
Subjects: LCSH: Squids--Juvenile fiction. | Moon--Juvenile fiction. | Confidence--Juvenile
    fiction. | Marine pollution--Juvenile fiction. | Picture books. | CYAC: Squids--Fiction. |
    Moon--Fiction. | Confidence--Fiction. | Marine pollution--Fiction.
Classification: LCC PZ10.3.P34 Li 2016 | DDC [E]--dc23

Printed and bound in the United States of America
First Edition | August 2016
10 9 8 7 6 5 4 3 2 1

www.padaleckistudio.com

PS

Little Moon

Story & Pictures by Megan Padalecki

On the far side of the reef, everything was perfectly still. Everything . . .

. . . but not the little egg.

Down

...and **down**

...and **down**

it went...

. . . to the very **deepest** place.

The little squid froze.
Nothing here felt right.

The cold was too cold.
The dark was too dark.
Even the water felt heavy and thick.

She had a **sinking feeling** -

– she was
Lost.

So the little squid set off to find a better fit . . .

. . . but did not get far.

At first she didn't know what to do.

She had never made ink before.

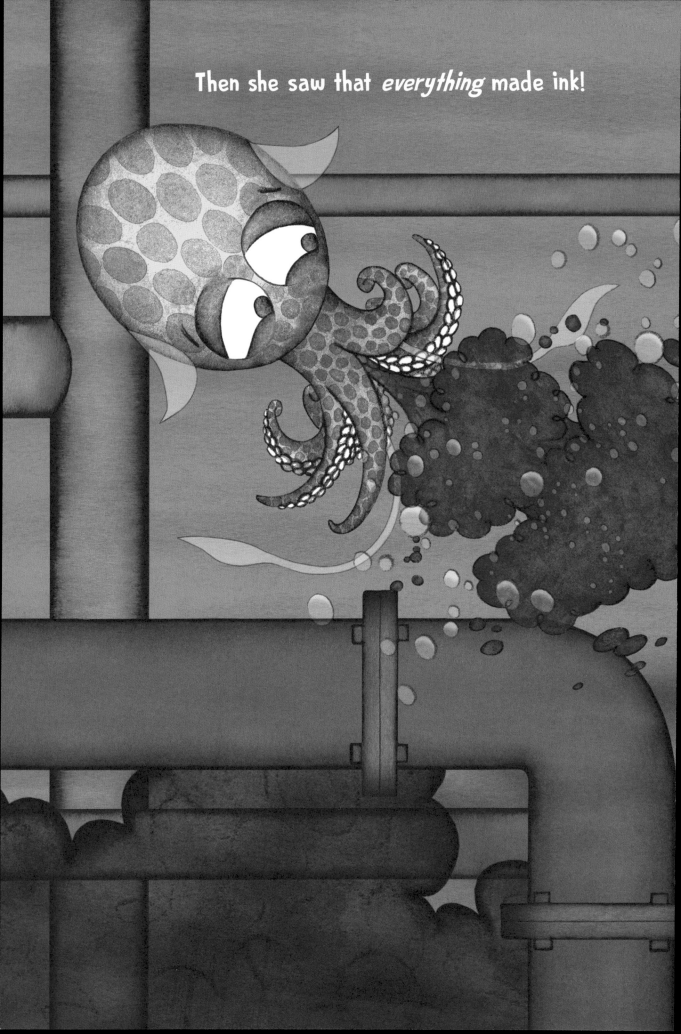

Then she saw that *everything* made ink!

And things started getting **messy** . . .

BIG MO
DRILLCO

She swam off with a big gulp –
and an even bigger sigh.

Many hours passed before she found anything.

But when she did, it seemed strangely familiar.

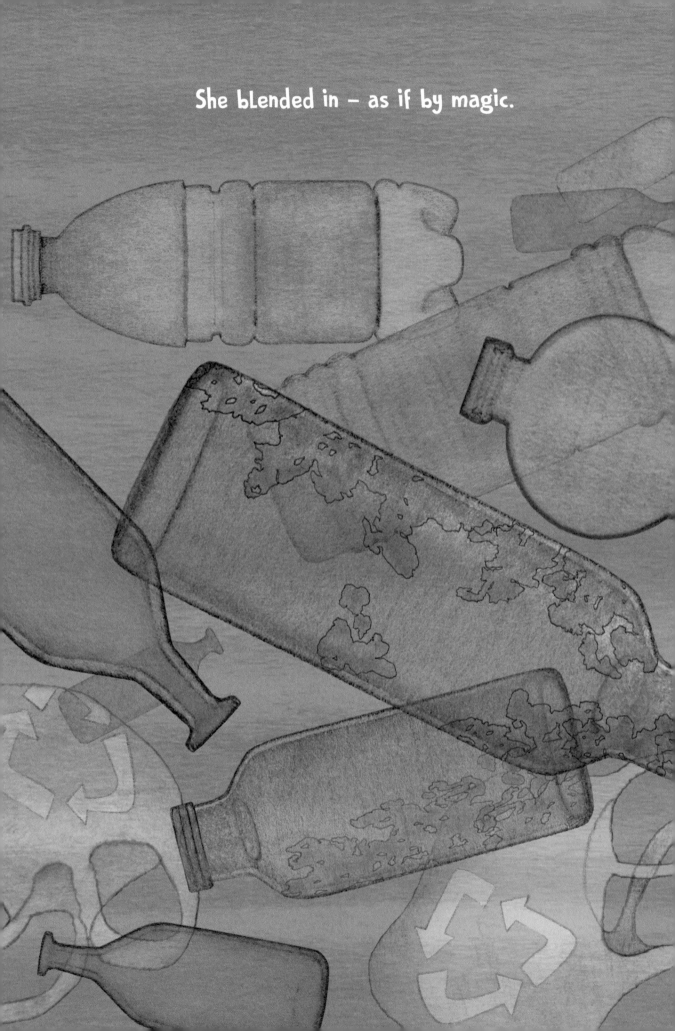

She blended in – as if by magic.

And the crowd **grew and grew** . . .

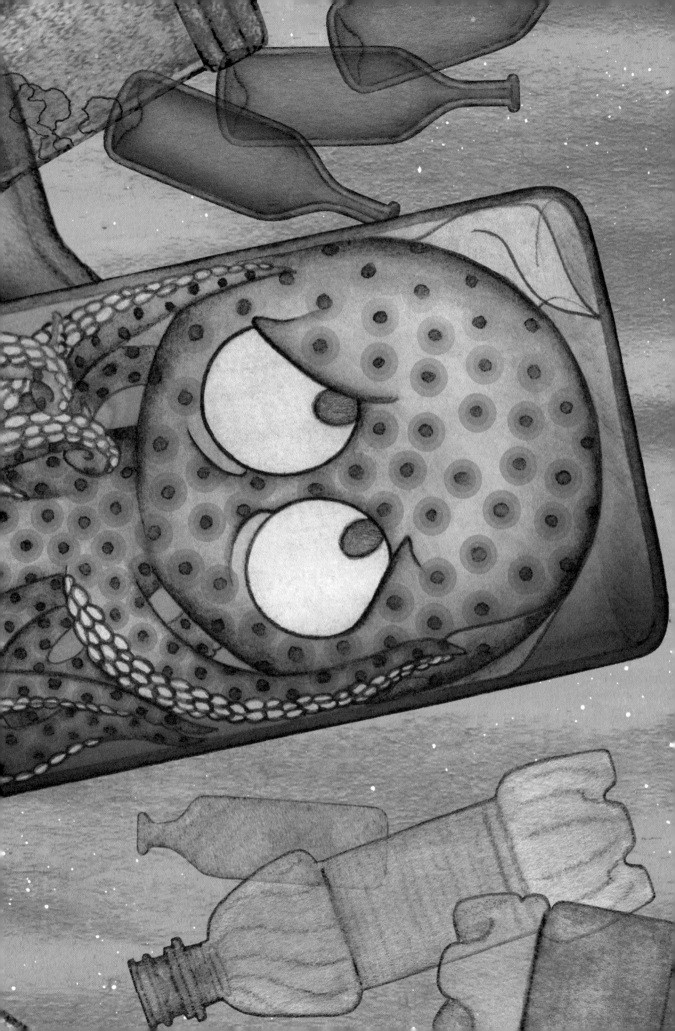

She swam away quickly –
and did not look back.

As night came, she wandered alone.

But not for long.

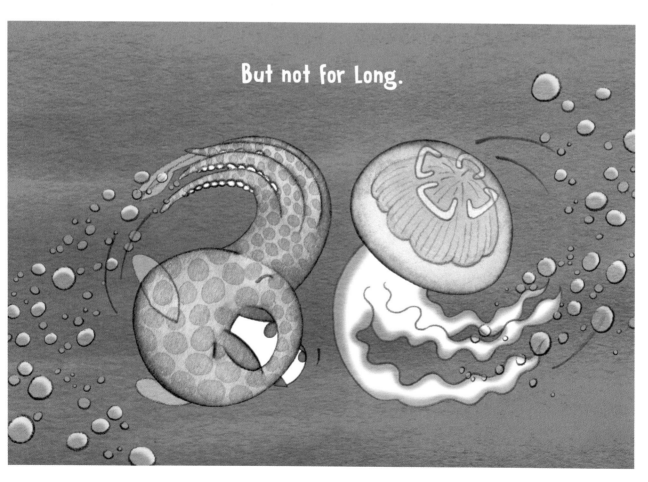

She joined the drifters in a silent dance.

Until she was
spotted . . .

She wanted to be noticed –
just not like THAT.

When it was too dark to see, she could only think.

She had come so far.
She had found so much.
But she still felt lost.

The little squid slumped into a sad ball.

Then something above urged her to **Lighten up.**

Under the moonlight, deep inside her squishy core . . .

. . . something SPARKED!

She had a good feeling.
Wherever that light was –

– that's where she
beLonged!

But the moon slipped away, and she was **on her own** again.

Only THIS time, her world didn't seem so dark.

So . . . she **DIPPED!**

And FLIPPED!

And **CHARGED** through unknown waters.

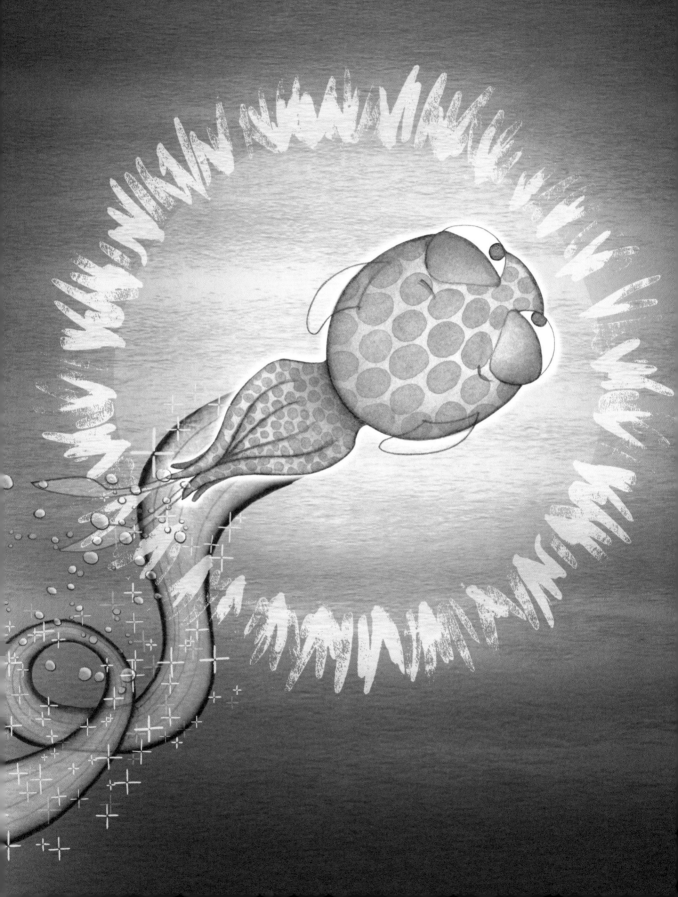

She **ZIPPED** past clever hunters.

And faced many night creatures . . .

. . . until she found the place that felt **JUST RIGHT**.

The little squid was the
brightest in her bunch.
And in the reef. And in the sea.

They called her **Moon**. And she beamed on.

About this Book

Illustrations for this book were hand-painted with watercolor pencils (Ivory Black) and watercolors (Prussian Blue). Final images were digitally colored and composed.

Text was set in Prince Frog and display type was derived from Lobster Two. The story was printed on 70 lb Husky Woodfree paper with 95 percent opacity.

The author's first book is *Big Mo*. This is her second.

. . . and this Character

The Hawaiian Bobtail Squid (*Euprymna scolopes*) lives in the shallow waters off the Hawaiian islands. It has eight suckered arms AND two special tentacles and is no bigger than your thumb. Please do not mistake one for an octopus!

For protection, this tiny cephalopod can change color and pattern and can squirt ink to confuse predators. It swims by jet propulsion and uses its fins to flip and dart.

The bobtail squid is active at night when it collects bioluminescent bacteria (*Vibrio fischeri*) that glow to blend perfectly with the moonlight. Without these glowing bacteria, predators would see the squid's silhouette and enjoy a tasty meal.

The author finds the bobtail squid to be very adorable and courageous.

. . . and our Ocean

The ocean is a vast and complex ecosystem, but it is still greatly affected by our human actions. There is always much more to discover below its calm surface.

On her journey, Moon is impacted by deepwater drilling, discarded trash, and warming waters (where slimy things like jellyfish thrive). The ocean can be a scary place for a little squid, even more so now than ever.

We are all responsible for protecting and conserving the miraculous life in our ocean! Find out how at ThankYouOcean.org/kid-zone/